HELPING YOUR BRAND-NEW READER

Here's how to make first-time reading easy and fun:

▶ Read the introduction at the beginning of the book aloud. Look through the pictures together so that your child can see what happens in the story before reading the words.

▶ Read the first page to your child, placing your finger under each word.

▶ Let your child touch the words and read the rest of the story. Give him or her time to figure out each new word.

▶ If your child gets stuck on a word, you might say, *"Try something. Look at the picture. What would make sense?"*

▶ If your child is still stuck, supply the right word. This will allow him or her to continue to read and enjoy the story. You might say, *"Could this word be 'ball'?"*

▶ Always praise your child. Praise what he or she reads correctly, and praise good tries too.

▶ Give your child lots of chances to read the story again and again. The more your child reads, the more confident he or she will become.

▶ Have fun!

First edition 2000

Library of Congress Cataloging-in-Publication Data
Hennessy, B. G. (Barbara G.)
Meet Dinah Dinosaur / B. G. Hennessy ;
illustrated by Ana Martín Larrañaga — 1st ed.
p.   cm. — (Brand new readers)
Summary: Presents the adventures of a playful
dinosaur for beginning readers.
ISBN 0-7636-1133-6
[1. Dinosaurs—Fiction.] I. Martín Larrañaga, Ana, date, ill. II. Title.
PZ7.H3914   Mc 2000
[E]—dc21   00-020927

2 4 6 8 10 9 7 5 3 1

Printed in Hong Kong

This book was typeset in Letraset Arta.
The illustrations were done in watercolor, pastel, and ink.

Candlewick Press
2067 Massachusetts Avenue
Cambridge, Massachusetts 02140

MEET DINAH DINOSAUR

CANDLEWICK PRESS
CAMBRIDGE, MASSACHUSETTS

B.G. Hennessy ILLUSTRATED BY **Ana Martín Larrañaga**

Contents

Dinah Likes to Eat 1

Little and Big 11

Hide and Seek 21

Dinah's Dream 31

DINAH LIKES TO EAT

Introduction

This story is called *Dinah Likes to Eat.*
It's about all the different things little
Dinah Dinosaur likes to eat.

3

Dinah Dinosaur likes to eat.

4

She eats little leaves.

She eats big leaves.

She eats yellow flowers.

She eats red flowers.

8

She eats purple flowers.

9

She eats and eats and eats.

But she's still a little dinosaur.

LITTLE AND BIG

Introduction

This story is called *Little and Big*.
It's about all the little and big things
Dinah Dinosaur finds, including
one that surprises her.

13

Dinah Dinosaur sees a little bird.

She sees a big bird.

15

She sees a little tree.

She sees a big tree.

17

She sees a little hole.

She does NOT see the big hole.

She falls in.

20

OUCH!

HIDE AND SEEK

Introduction

This story is called *Hide and Seek*. It's about how Dinah Dinosaur and her friend Doug play and get messier and messier, until they are so messy that Doug can't find Dinah.

23

Dinah and Doug are friends.

They swim in the water.

They sit in the mud.

They run in the grass.

They roll in the sand.

They jump in the leaves.

They play hide and seek.

30

But Doug can't find Dinah.

DINAH'S DREAM

Introduction

This story is called *Dinah's Dream*.
It's about how Dinah Dinosaur goes
to sleep and dreams she is different
things, until she wakes up.

33

Dinah Dinosaur goes to sleep.

34

She dreams she is a fish.

35

She dreams she is a girl.

She dreams she is a dog.

37

She dreams she is a bird.

38

She dreams she is flying.

CRASH!

40

Dinah Dinosaur wakes up.